These are the last days of the Library of Doom.

The forces of villainy are freeing the Library's most dangerous books. Only one thing can stop Evil from penning history's final chapter – the League of Librarians, a mysterious collection of heroes who only appear when the Library faces its greatest threat.

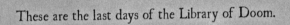

Never underestimate the power of words.

THESAURUS REX

By Michael Dahl

Illustrated by
Bradford Kendall

Raintree is an imprint of Capstone Global Library Limited, a company
incorporated in England and Wales having its registered office at 7
Pilgrim Street, London, EC4V 6LB – Registered company number: 6695582

www.raintree.co.uk
myorders@raintree.co.uk

Designed by Hilary Wacholz
Original illustrations © Capstone 2016
Illustrated by Bradford Kendall
ISBN 978 1 4747 1057 2 (paperback)
20 19 18 17 16
10 9 8 7 6 5 4 3 2 1

British Library Cataloguing in Publication Data
A full catalogue record for this book is available from
the British Library.

Printed and bound in China.

CONTENTS

Chapter 1

JURASSIC GREED

Lizzy checks the library shelves. All the dinosaur books are **MISSING**.

She walks to the front desk of the public library. *The assistant will know where they are,* she thinks.

She waits in line behind a boy. His name is Cooper. He has green hair.

Lizzy **glances** at the pile of books in front of him. All of them are about dinosaurs.

"You can't check out all those books!" Lizzy says.

"There's no book limit," Cooper says. "Anyway, I need them for my project. It's on the Jurassic period."

The clerk pushes the books towards Cooper. He **STUFFS** them into his rucksack.

"But I also have to do my dinosaur project," Lizzy says. "I need those books too."

Cooper shrugs. "That's not my problem," he says. Cooper throws his rucksack over a shoulder. He walks away.

Without looking back, the green-haired boy waves goodbye to Lizzy.

Chapter 2

MISPRINT?

The library is about to close. Lizzy checks row after row. None of the shelves have dinosaur books.

She rubs her chin. "I can't write much about dinosaurs without books," she says. "I suppose I'll just have to use lots of extra words!"

At school, Lizzy once used a thesaurus to find new words. The library has to have one, she thinks.

Lizzy hurries down a **DARK**, narrow aisle. All the books are big.

"Ah! There it is," she says.

Lizzy kneels down. She grabs a book on the bottom shelf.

The cover of the book feels like alligator skin.

The book's title is also strange.

THE SAURUS

Why is there a gap in the middle of the word? she wonders. *It must be a misprint.*

Chapter 3

GULP

That night, Lizzy stays up late. She sits at a table in her bedroom. The **thesaurus** is open in front of her.

Lizzy knows she has to get up early. She has lots of chores to do before she catches the school bus. But she has to finish her project first.

She takes a drink from her glass of water.

Suddenly, the table **shakes**. The glass
tips over. Water spills on the open pages.

The water quickly soaks into the paper.

Then it disappears. The pages are dry.

Lizzy hears a strange gulping sound.
It seems to be coming from the book.

"That's weird," she says.

Chapter 4

THE SAURUS

Suddenly, the book's pages flap wildly.

Lizzy jumps up and **SCREAMS**.

The book flies into the air. It soars out
of an open window.

FWOOSH!

The book drops into the darkness outside.

Lizzy looks out of the window. The book lays open on the wet grass. The pages begin to unfold.

They fit together. They become a **GIANT** ball of paper.

The ball bulges out. It expands.

It takes the shape of a dinosaur.

ROAR!

A papery T-Rex glares up at Lizzy's window.

Lizzy hears her mother scream.

Her father runs out onto the lawn. Dad holds
a hunting rifle. He aims at the dinosaur.

Lizzy sees a word form on the creature's chest.

BULLETPROOF

Her father fires his rifle. BANG!

The T-Rex roars. The bullets **bounce** off his paper hide.

Lizzy sees more words. They form on the wrinkled paper skin.

The dinosaur shifts its **HUNGRY** gaze to Lizzy's father.

Chapter 5

GENRE CHANGING

Lightning rips across the night sky.

A strange man appears on the grass.

He wears silver glasses. His inky, long coat **shines** in the moonlight.

The man faces the creature. He raises his arms towards the T-Rex.

Lightning bolts **BLAST** from his fingers.

The blast hits the creature's powerful chest.

The creature screams. It crumples up like a wet, paper bag.

The **strange** man looks up. He sees Lizzy in the window.

"Don't worry," he says.

Lizzie points. "Look out!" she cries.

The giant, crumpled pages begin to unfold.

The paper shifts swiftly. The pages take the shape of a gigantic scorpion.

A spike grows from its glowing body. Horns sprout from its head.

The monster lifts its **spiked** tail. It aims at the man.

The man rolls across the grass.

FOOM!

The **DEADLY** blow just misses him. The stranger points at the creature.

More lightning bursts from his fingers.

Again, the monster screams. Again, it crumples up. And again, it unfolds into a new monster.

The creature stretches out its **tentacles**. It lets out an otherworldly cry.

Lizzie sees a new word appear on its body.

ALIEN.

"It keeps changing genres!" says the man.

The man raises his arms. He aims at the grass. "So I must change the context!" he says.

Electricity shoots from his hands. *ZZZZZRRRRT!*

A circle of flame rises up.

The paper monster is surrounded.

Lizzy watches as a new word appears,
over and over, on the wrinkled hide.

FLAMMABLE

The monster's paper edges catch fire.

Thick smoke engulfs the lawn.

Soon, the creature is gone. All that's left is a **pile** of ash.

The man gathers the covers of the thesaurus. "These must go back to my Library," he says.

Then he steps into the billowing smoke. And vanishes.

Just then, a car drives up to the house. It screeches to a stop.

A green-haired boy jumps out.

"Lizzy!" Cooper shouts. "What's happened? I heard all this noise!"

Lizzy points at the pile of smoking ash.

"Homework," she says. "It's a real **BEAST!**"

GLOSSARY

aisle passage where people walk

context words that are used with a certain word or phrase and that help to explain its meaning

gaze look at someone or something in a steady way and usually for a long time

genre particular type or category of literature or art

Jurassic from a period of the Mesozoic Epoch, occurring from 190 to 140 million years ago, featuring many kinds of dinosaurs

misprint spelling mistake in something that is printed

otherworldly alien, not of this world, or amazingly different

thesaurus book in which words that have the same or similar meanings are grouped together

DISCUSSION QUESTIONS

1. With each word that appears on the Thesaurus Rex, the beast takes on the word's qualities. What kinds of words would have been even more effective at defeating the Librarian?

2. Discuss the words that the monster showed on its chest. For each word, think of some ways the Librarian could have defeated the monster based on the words it used.

3. In what ways might a thesaurus be useful for studying? What about for writing? Discuss thesauruses.

WRITING PROMPTS

1. Create your own heroic word monster. What does it look like? How does it use words to defeat evil? Write about it, then draw a picture of your monster.

2. Create a list of your favourite words. Then write a short story using as many of them as you can.

3. Origami is the Japanese art of folding paper. What shapes would you have chosen for the monster to take? Write about the monster shape-shifting into other forms.

THE AUTHOR

Michael Dahl is the prolific author of the bestselling *Goodnight, Baseball* picture book and more than 200 other books for children and young adults. He has won the AEP Distinguished Achievement Award three times for his non fiction, a Teachers' Choice Award from *Learning* magazine and a Seal of Excellence from the Creative Child Awards. He is also the author of the Hocus Pocus Hotel mystery series and the Dragonblood books. Dahl currently lives in Minnesota, USA.

THE ILLUSTRATOR

Bradford Kendall has enjoyed drawing for as long as he can remember. As a boy, he loved to read comic books and watch old monster movies. He graduated from the Rhode Island School of Design with a BFA in Illustration. He has owned his own commercial art business since 1983. Bradford lives in Rhode Island, USA, with his wife, Leigh, and their two children, Lily and Stephen.